First Biographies
Molly Pitcher

by Jan Mader

Consulting Editor: Gail Saunders-Smith, PhD

Consultant: Dr. David G. Martin
Author, *A Molly Pitcher Sourcebook*

Capstone
press®

Mankato, Minnesota

Pebble Books are published by Capstone Press,
1710 Roe Crest Drive, North Mankato, Minnesota 56003.
www.capstonepress.com

Library of Congress Cataloging-in-Publication Data
Mader, Jan.
   Molly Pitcher / by Jan Mader.
   p. cm.—(Pebble books. First biographies)
   Summary: "Simple text and photographs present the legend of Molly
Pitcher"—Provided by publisher.
   Includes bibliographical references and index.
   ISBN-13: 978-0-7368-6703-0 (hardcover)
   ISBN-10: 0-7368-6703-1 (hardcover)
   ISBN-13: 978-0-7368-7843-2 (softcover)
   ISBN-10: 0-7368-7843-2 (softcover)
   1. Pitcher, Molly, 1754–1832—Juvenile literature. 2. Monmouth, Battle of,
Freehold, N.J., 1778—Juvenile literature. 3. United States—History—Revolution,
1775–1783—Women—Juvenile literature. 4. United States—History—Revolution,
1775–1783—Biography—Juvenile literature. I. Title. II. Series.
E241.M7M29 2007
973.3'34092—dc22   2006020933

Note to Parents and Teachers

The First Biographies set supports national history standards for
units on people and culture. This book describes and illustrates
the legend of Molly Pitcher. The images support early readers in
understanding the text. The repetition of words and phrases helps
early readers learn new words. This book also introduces early
readers to subject-specific vocabulary words, which are defined
in the Glossary section. Early readers may need assistance to read
some words and to use the Table of Contents, Glossary, Read More,
Internet Sites, and Index sections of the book.

Table of Contents

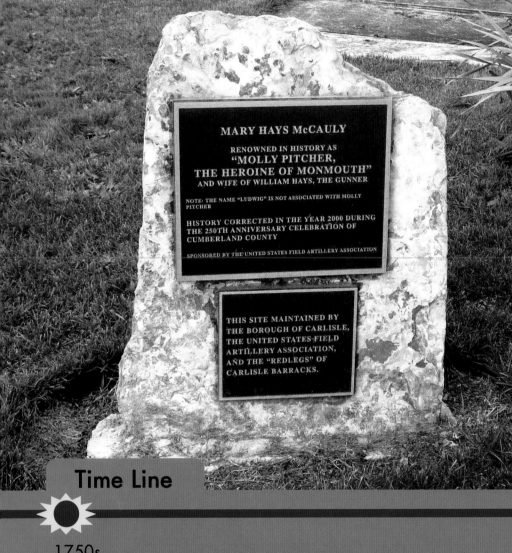

MARY HAYS McCAULY

RENOWNED IN HISTORY AS
**"MOLLY PITCHER,
THE HEROINE OF MONMOUTH"**
AND WIFE OF WILLIAM HAYS, THE GUNNER

NOTE: THE NAME "LUDWIG" IS NOT ASSOCIATED WITH MOLLY PITCHER

HISTORY CORRECTED IN THE YEAR 2000 DURING THE 250TH ANNIVERSARY CELEBRATION OF CUMBERLAND COUNTY

SPONSORED BY THE UNITED STATES FIELD ARTILLERY ASSOCIATION

THIS SITE MAINTAINED BY THE BOROUGH OF CARLISLE, THE UNITED STATES-FIELD ARTILLERY ASSOCIATION, AND THE "REDLEGS" OF CARLISLE BARRACKS.

Time Line

1750s
born

The Legend

Molly Pitcher is an American legend. Some people believe Mary Hays McCauly was the real Molly Pitcher. Mary Hays was born in the 1750s in Pennsylvania.

 monument in the town where Mary was born

5

Time Line

1750s
born

1769
marries
William Hays

1775
Revolutionary
War begins

The War Begins

In 1769, Mary married William Hays.
The Revolutionary War began in 1775.
America went to war with Great Britain.
William was a soldier.

Battle of Concord Bridge at the start of the war

Time Line

1750s
born

1769
marries
William Hays

1775
Revolutionary
War begins

At the time, women could not be soldiers. But Mary wanted to help. She lived in a camp with other women near the battles.

 women living in a Revolutionary War camp

Time Line

1750s
born

1769
marries
William Hays

1775
Revolutionary
War begins

Mary and the other women took care of the soldiers. The soldiers called all the women Molly. Molly was a common nickname.

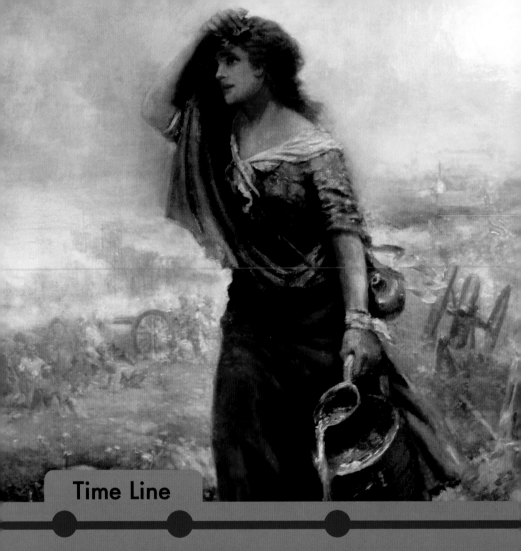

Time Line

1750s
born

1769
marries
William Hays

1775
Revolutionary
War begins

Molly Pitcher

When it was hot,
soldiers cried out for water.
Mary brought them pitchers
of water from a nearby well.
The soldiers started calling
her Molly Pitcher.

Time Line

1750s
born

1769
marries
William Hays

1775
Revolutionary
War begins

14

In 1778, William was hurt
in a battle.
Mary took over his cannon.
She loaded it
and fired it herself.
Mary was a hero.

 Molly during the Battle of Monmouth in 1778

1778
takes over
cannon

Time Line

1750s
born

1769
marries
William Hays

1775
Revolutionary
War begins

After the war, soldiers told
stories about Molly Pitcher.
Molly's name became
a symbol of the women
who helped during
the Revolutionary War.

1778
takes over
cannon

1783
Revolutionary
War ends

Time Line

1750s
born

1769
marries
William Hays

1775
Revolutionary
War begins

18

Mary Hays went back
to Pennsylvania.
She told stories about
the war. In 1822,
the government gave Mary
money for her help
during the war.

 George Washington thanking Molly Pitcher

1778
takes over
cannon

1783
Revolutionary
War ends

1822
receives
money

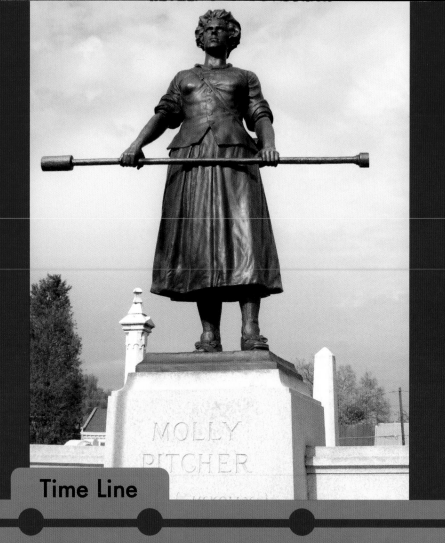

Time Line

1750s
born

1769
marries
William Hays

1775
Revolutionary
War begins

Honoring Molly

Mary died in 1832.
Today, a statue in Mary's
hometown honors her
as Molly Pitcher.

1778
takes over
cannon

1783
Revolutionary
War ends

1822
receives
money

1832
dies

Glossary

hero—a brave person who people look up to or admire

honor—to show respect or give praise to someone for something they've done

legend—a story passed down from earlier times; it is hard to prove if legends are true.

nickname—a name used instead of a person's real name; Molly was a nickname given to many women during the 1700s.

pitcher—a container for liquid that has an open top, handle, and a spout

Revolutionary War—the war that helped America win its freedom from Great Britain; the war started in 1775 and ended in 1783.

symbol—a person or object that reminds people of something else; the story of Molly Pitcher reminds people of all the women who worked hard during the Revolutionary War.

Read More

Dahl, Michael. *Bring Us Water, Molly Pitcher!: A Fun Song about the Battle of Monmouth.* Fun Songs. Minneapolis: Picture Window Books, 2004.

Poulakidas, Georgene. *The American Revolutionary War.* Primary Sources of American Wars. New York: PowerKids Press, 2006.

Internet Sites

FactHound offers a safe, fun way to find Internet sites related to this book. All of the sites on FactHound have been researched by our staff.

Here's how:

1. Visit *www.facthound.com*

2. Choose your grade level.

3. Type in this book ID **0736867031** for age-appropriate sites. You may also browse subjects by clicking on letters, or by clicking on pictures and words.

4. Click on the **Fetch It** button.

FactHound will fetch the best sites for you!

Index

Word Count: 208
Grades: 1–2
Early-Intervention Level: 24

Editorial Credits
Sarah L. Schuette, editor; Mary Bode, book designer; Wanda Winch, photo
    researcher/photo editor

Photo Credits
Capstone Press/Kim Brown, cover
Corbis/Bettmann, 10
Dennis Malone Carter, Molly Pitcher Presented to General Washington, Oil
    on canvas, dated 1856, The Monmouth County Historical Assoc., Freehold, N.J.,
    gift of Mrs. J. Armory Haskell, 1941, 18
Edward Percy Moran, Molly Pitcher at Monmouth, oil on canvas, early 20th century, used
    by permission of Charles Glenn May, 12
Library of Congress, 1
North Wind Picture Archives, 14; Nancy Carter, 4, 20
Pamela Patrick White, www.ppatrickwhite.com, 8, 16
SuperStock, 6